Harriet Ziefert

MURPHY JUMPS A HURDLE

Illustrated by Emily Bolam

BLUE APPLE BOOKS

For Will

Text copyright © 2006 by Harriet Ziefert
Illustrations copyright © 2006 by Emily Bolam
All rights reserved / CIP Data is available.
Published in the United States 2006 by
Blue Apple Books
P.O. Box 1380, Maplewood, N.J. 07040
www.blueapplebooks.com
Distributed in the U.S. by Chronicle Books
Printed in China
First Edition
ISBN 13: 978-1-59354-174-3
ISBN 10: 1-59354-174-0
1 3 5 7 9 10 8 6 4 2

I'm Murphy. Everyone says I'm handsome.
Everyone says I'm fit!

I work out with Cheryl every day.
Today we're doing twenty minutes on the treadmill.

I used to be fat. Too much food and too little exercise—
that's what did it. After I lost twelve pounds,
Cheryl decided that agility training was for us.

She checked it out on the Internet
and found a place where
we could train.

Here I am weaving around poles.
This is harder than it looks.
I'm supposed to enter with the first pole to my left,
then weave in and out, not skipping any.

"Fault!" yells Cheryl.
"You skipped a pole!"

I also practice on the A-frame.

I climb up one side and down the other.

The teeter-totter is my favorite.
It only takes me about two seconds
to hit the ground running!

After a workout, I'm happy to chill out on
the front porch and watch the people go by.

But Cheryl usually
comes along and asks,
"Want to play Fetch?"

She throws a wooden dumbbell.

I go straight for it.

Here I am sitting in front of Cheryl
waiting for her to tell me to release it.

I'll wait and try not to drop the dumbbell,
but I sure wish she'd hurry up
and give me permission to let it go.

One Saturday morning Cheryl
shows me the newspaper.

She reads to me: *Dog Show Today.*
"Do you want to compete?"
she asks.

I am a little nervous, but I'd like to try. I wag my tail, Yes!

"Well, then," says Cheryl,
"you need to get cleaned up."

I have a bath . . .

and a brushing.

Cheryl even brushes my teeth.
I don't like toothbrushing,
but Cheryl says that nobody likes
a dog with bad breath.

On Saturday afternoon Cheryl loads me into the back of the station wagon and drives to the show.

I'd like to
win a ribbon.

Wish us luck!

The obstacle course is all set up.
The tunnel . . . the A-frame . . . the teeter-totter . . .
the weaving poles—they're all there.

I keep my nose in the air.
There are lots of dogs to smell.

COMPETITORS'
ENCLOSURE

Cheryl takes a short, walk-through
before the competition starts.
We're a team. She needs to figure
out how best to guide me
around the obstacles.

I wait impatiently and wonder,

What's taking her so long?

MURPHY
AND
CHERYL

There are six dogs competing in my group.
I will be the third to go.

The announcer says,
"Get ready for the team of Murphy and Cheryl."

We walk to the
starting line.

Cheryl gives me a signal
and I'm off!

across the plank . . .

down the A-frame . . .

in and out of the poles . . .

through the tunnel . . .

over the hurdle . . .

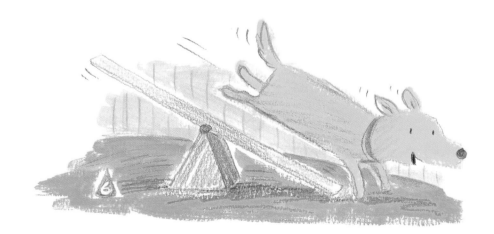

off the teeter-totter!

All the dogs and their handlers wait on the field
for the judge to announce the winners.

Cheryl says, "You were really
accurate, Murphy. No faults!
But I don't know about your speed.
We may not have been fast enough."

The judge reads the names and
the finishing times of the winners.

MURPHY
AND
CHERYL

"You got third place!" says Cheryl.
"Let's get your ribbon!"

I'm not happy with third place, but Cheryl
says it's really good for our first dog show.

3RD
PLACE

"Smile," says Cheryl.
"Our picture might be in the newspaper."

"Maybe we'll win first place next time,"
says Cheryl.

"Murphy, you're doing great!
How about a twenty-five minute
workout today?"

The End